THE

MOONS

OF

AUGUST

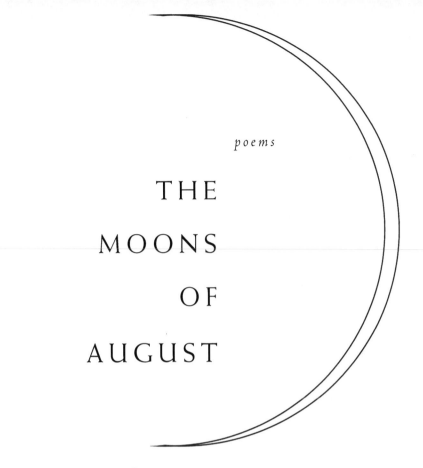

poems

THE

MOONS

OF

AUGUST

Danusha Laméris

Autumn House
Press

pittsburgh

"Autumn House" and "Autumn House Press" are registered trademarks owned by Autumn House Press, a nonprofit corporation whose mission is the publication and promotion of poetry and other fine literature.

Autumn House Press Staff
Michael Simms: Founder and Editor-in-Chief
Eva Simms: Co-Founder and President
Giuliana Certo: Managing Editor
Christine Stroud: Associate Editor
Sharon Dilworth, John Fried: Fiction Editors
J.J. Bosley, CPA: Treasurer
Anne Burnham: Fundraising Consultant
Michael Wurster: Community Outreach Consultant
Jan Beatty: Media Consultant
Heather Cazad: Contest Consultant
Michael Milberger: Tech Crew Chief
Chris Duerr: Intern

Autumn House Press receives state arts funding support through a grant from the Pennsylvania Council on the Arts, a state agency funded by the Commonwealth of Pennsylvania, and the National Endowment for the Arts, a federal agency.

ISBN: 978-1-932870-95-4
Library of Congress Control Number: 2013950643

For my brother, Isma'il

and for my son, Santiago

"...And we talk
as if death were a line to be crossed.
Look at them, the white roses.
Tell me where they end."

—*Mark Doty, "Beach Roses"*

CONTENTS

Before

three

four

THE
MOONS
OF
AUGUST

The table still set.
The goblets filled with wine.
Her body lean, taut as a birch.
The gifts not yet given.

That which will be torn remains whole.
The heart, unbroken.
The mother alive, setting out the dishes.

one

I don't remember the sounds
rising from below my breastbone
though I spoke that golden language
with the girls of Beirut. Playing hopscotch
on the hot asphalt, we called out to our mothers
for lemonade, and when the men
walking home from work stooped down,
slipped us coins for candy, we thanked them.
At the market, I understood the bargaining
of the butcher, the vendors of fig and bread.
In Arabic, I whispered into the tufted ears
of a donkey, professing my love. And in Arabic
I sang at school, or dreamt at night.
There is an Arab saying,
Sad are only those who understand.
What did I know then of the endless trail
of losses? In the years that have passed,
I've buried a lover, a brother, a son.
At night, the low drumroll
of bombs eroded the edges of the city.
The girls? Who knows what has been taken
from them.

For a brief season I woke
to a man who would whisper to me
in Arabic, then tap the valley of my sternum,
ask me to repeat each word,
coaxing the rusty syllables from my throat.
See he said, *they're still there.*

Though even that memory is faint.
And maybe he was right. What's gone
is not quite gone, but lingers.
Not the language, but the bones
of the language. Not the beloved,
but the dark bed the beloved makes
inside our bodies.

THE MOONS OF AUGUST

after Dorianne Laux

There are many names
for this sullied coin,
this brandy-soaked pearl:
Fruit Moon, Lightning Moon,
Moon When All Things Ripen.
We stand by the creek,
watch it float between the black
tips of the pine. Grain Moon,
Full Sturgeon Moon,
Green Corn Moon.
I count my losses in the dark.
Why not call it
Cracked Quartz Moon,
Roll of the Dice Moon,
Hard Luck Moon.
Must we always speak
of harvest? Crickets throb
in the dusky vines.
A bat flits above our heads.
Oh Watcher, you
who see all that is born
and all that dies
tonight I name you
Switchblade Moon,
Toss in the Towel Moon,
Moon Turning to Sand,
Empty Rice Bowl,
Dust Moon, Salt Moon,
Ash Moon,
Blink of an Eye Moon.

She would sink down
into the dirt
behind the house
wetness streaking
her face.
No other child like hers.

He ran wild,
always opening his mouth
before strangers.

Sometimes, at the well,
filling earthen jugs
with water
she thought of the night
she birthed him

the dark smell of hay
filling her lungs
the swirl of stars.

How she had died, then,
disappeared into blackness,
and was born with him,

his crown breaching
the tight seal of her flesh.

What light!
For a moment, she was sunrise
breaking over the horizon.

She was mountains, rivers
a quiet swath of forest
the quick movements of birds.

But now, there was only the crack
of Joseph's hammer
hitting dull nails
into a plank of wood

crows circling the carcass of a ewe,
dead that morning
the air hot and still
as held breath—
the child, where was he?

All day long we ambled down the sidewalks of Montréal
lined with bistros and beautiful women
leaning on wrought iron banisters,
our hair thick with humidity,
the smoke of cigarettes filling our lungs.
We ate skinny fries and stared at each other through the haze,
our vows still shiny as the silverware.
My cousin's boyfriend was a painter.
We teased him about his work, the paintings white,
all of them. Though, as he showed us,
different textures. Some smooth, subtly altered,
like maps describing the craters of the moon.
At night, when the sky emptied its purse
of silver coins on the tin roof, we curled up together
in the narrow bed and watched lightning thread the dark.
Now, we sit across from one another in the pediatric ward,
playing Scrabble, jotting down the scores
in a wire-bound notebook,
exhausted, eyeing the last scraps
of a ham sandwich from the cafeteria
while our son sleeps in his metal cot,
rubber tubes snaking in and out of his body.
Coming and going, sleeping on benches in the hallway,
ducking into fluorescent bathrooms
before morning doctors' meetings.
Years like this.

Awake, he wasn't like the other babies.
His dark eyes shifted, jittered.
Sometimes the wispy hair
stood entirely on end, electric.

Asleep, swaddled,
he seemed almost one of them.
His breath steady
fingers curled against his palm.

I prayed the bad god
wouldn't see him there,
would pass by, leave me this boy
with the peach skin face, a lash fallen on his cheek.

I could have slipped him home, safely,
bundled in that worn blanket, taken him
across the threshold
into that other, waiting life.

To bless once meant to draw blood
as with the tip of a blade,
blessing, the act of wounding.
And now it has come to mean
a cutting through what cannot be seen
the way a saint might pass her hand,
over the bent head of a supplicant.
Or how a mother begins to weep
as her newborn is handed to her for the first time.

Is ordinary goodness more than we can bear?

Lovers have the name of the beloved
pierced into their flesh, their pleasure so unbearable
only the point of a needle can say
what ecstasy they suffer.

The minister prays over the newlyweds
may you be blessed all your days
yet we know they will be wounded
by each other. We count our blessings,
the ways life has broken
us. *Hail Mary, blessed among women,*
weeping at the feet of her only son.

What a blessing to be alive, we say
knowing this life is so unlikely, so near impossible
that it is a blessing to be born at all,
to come into this world wailing,
covered in blood.

WHEN HE FATTENED UP

I always felt better when he fattened up
the folds of his wrists and elbows
proof of the rich milk.
I could have danced around the room,
thrown streamers from the top window.

It almost didn't matter
that I had to pipe red liquid from a syringe
into his cheek each morning and night,
that the doctors shrugged and shook their heads.

We had triumphed in the most basic of things:
he had accepted my milk, taken it into his body.

And now he looked tremendous, content
like the Buddha after he'd
sat beneath the Bodhi Tree
and warded off the demons.
After he'd transcended the world.

What was this sound—
    man or woman?
        It could have been
    wind
rubbing branches
    against the window.
My mother laid down
    the furrowed disk, and up
it lifted, this voice,
        not angel
nor demon
    but something elemental
    that set itself deep
in my marrow.
        Burnt sugar
makes caramel,
crushed grapes, wine.
    What sorrows, distilled,
this woeful cadence?
      I could close
my eyes
    and feel it pour over me,
      something sweet
and perilous.
    Oracle. Harbinger.

    Teller of things,
what is it I'll need to know—
      You who went ahead
    and lived.

I HAVE BEEN THAT WOMAN

I have been that woman
in the loose dress
wandering the halls of the hospital
her body still torn from birth.

I have sat over a blue, plastic tray
a carton of juice, a sandwich
given to nursing mothers.

I saw my child's soft, new veins
pierced again and again,
an IV taped to his forehead,
watched the doctors drop their eyes
when I asked if he would live.

So even though I sit here
looking out at the trees,
the pale evening sky,

she lives in me still
her unkempt hair—
the dry taste in her mouth
her breasts filling slowly with milk.

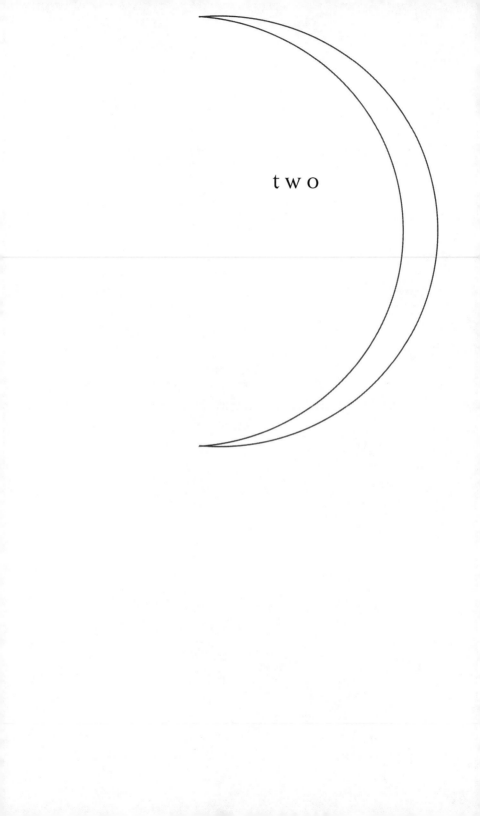

two

INSHA'ALLAH

I don't know when it slipped into my speech
that soft word meaning, "if God wills it."
Insha'Allah I will see you next summer.
The baby will come in spring, insha'Allah.
Insha'Allah this year we will have enough rain.

So many plans I've laid have unraveled
easily as braids beneath my mother's quick fingers.

Every language must have a word for this. A word
our grandmothers uttered under their breath
as they pinned the whites, soaked in lemon,
hung them to dry in the sun, or peeled potatoes,
dropping the discarded skins into a bowl.

Our sons will return next month, insha'Allah.
Insha'Allah this war will end, soon. Insha'Allah
the rice will be enough to last through winter.

How lightly we learn to hold hope,
as if it were an animal that could turn around
and bite your hand. And still we carry it
the way a mother would, carefully,
from one day to the next.

This one thinks, let me be the slender bow
of the violin. Another, the body of the instrument,
burnished amber.

One imagines life as a narrow boat
crossing water,
a light mist of salt on the prow.

And still another—planed down to planks,
then hammered into shelter
voices vibrating through the rafters.

We do not notice their pleasure,
the slight hum of the banister
beneath our palms,

the satisfaction of the desk
as we tap our pens, impatiently,
upon its weathered surface.

They have ferried us
across rough seas
to lands that smelled of cinnamon,

carried arrowheads to pierce our enemies,
housed our senators,
who pace the creaky floors, debating.

We have boiled their pulp,
pressed it into thin,
white sheets of paper.

And when we die,
they meet us in the blackened soil
and take us back

carry us
up the length of their bodies
into the trembling leaves.

What happens to the ones that fall out of favor:
the Dorises and Archibalds,
the Theodores and Eunices?
They all had their day,
once roamed the earth in multitudes
alongside Gerties and Wyatts—
at least one in every classroom.
Names written in neat block print,
scratched into tree bark,
engraved on heart-shaped lockets,
filling the morning paper
with weddings and engagements.
How could they have known
that one-by-one the Constances
and Clydes would disappear,
replaced by Jennifers, Jacobs,
Ashleys and Aidens.
That few would ever dance again,
corsages pinned to their breasts
or hear their names on the radio
whispered in dedication,
or uttered in darkness
by a breathless voice,
or even shouted out in anger—
"Seymour!"—
as they grabbed the keys and stormed out the door.
Each name fading quietly from daily life

as though it had never existed,
except for the letters etched into stone,
warmed by the sun
and at night, lit by a crescent moon.

Did she know
there was more to life
than lions licking the furred
ears of lambs,
fruit trees dropping
their fat bounty,
the years droning on
without argument?

Too much quiet
is never a good sign.
Isn't there always
something itching
beneath the surface?

But what could she say?
The larder was full
and they were beautiful,
their bodies new
as the day they were made.

Each morning the same
flowers broke through
the rich soil, the birds sang,
again, in perfect pitch.

It was only at night
when they lay together in the dark

that it was almost palpable—
the vague sadness, unnamed.

Foolishness, betrayal,
—call it what you will. What a relief
to feel the weight
fall into her palm. And after,
not to pretend anymore
that the terrible calm
was Paradise.

One, tossed to Aphrodite,
begins a war. Eve, that fateful bite
into the crisp red skin.
Distracted by the sight of golden apples
a virgin huntress loses a race
and must marry. Each apple
a kind of failure. The body
calling out desire. Isn't there
always something we want
more than our own happiness?
A pull toward the Fall.
Haven't we all loved too much?
Snow White bit into the flesh
laced with poison.
Love is something we fall into.
Fall, the time of ripening apples.
In England one *falls* pregnant.
Life requires collapse
holds it out to us
sweet and fragrant.

Sixty-two years since the last sighting,
ornithologists say they've spotted one
somewhere along the lip of the White River
its pale beak, red crest, black and white feathered tuxedo,
the last of the ivory-billed woodpeckers.
Could it be, they wonder
that the birds have gone deeper,
nested in the southern bottomland?
People kept killing them
to show in museums
nailing their bodies to planks.
Now the town is buzzing with tourists
armed with binoculars.
Isn't this how it is? We want back
what we've taken, the way a child tries
to set the head back on a doll.
Houdini underwater, escaping the chained suitcase,
Jesus risen in white robes
standing outside the door to his grave.
We destroy what we desire:
the lithe and fearsome tiger,
humans adorned in feathers and the skins of bison,
entire forests, quiet as cathedrals.
And then we want it back,
that thin strip of green, lush again,
the Lord God Bird, as it was known
set back on its branch,
scaling bald patches into the rough bark.

These hundred or so graceless travelers
swarm and caw,
thicken the peach blossom sky,
then dive downward
to land on the thin, black wires.

Below, the dusty road,
an old tractor
late light glinting
off its fender.

What urgency
has brought them here,
these messengers,
their cacophony of barbed voices?

Maybe they're the Dead
returned, come to tell us
they're not elsewhere, but here,
between the low cloud layer
and rotting loam.

That while we mourn for them,
all along they have been
calling back to us
in their loudest, harshest songs.

Because they crowd the corner
of every city street,
because they are the color
of sullied steel,
because they scavenge,
eating every last crust,
we do not favor them.

They raise their young
huddled under awnings
above the liquor store

circle our feet, pecking at crumbs
pace the sidewalk
with that familiar strut.

None will ever attain greatness.
Though every once in a while
in a tourist's blurry snapshot
of a grand cathedral

they rise into the pale gray sky
all at once.

This morning I looked out the window
and saw their small, translucent pelts
hanging from the boughs. For months, the birds
have been feasting: flickers, finches, scrub jays.
And now, the fruit cleaned of itself, laid bare,
light shining through the last scraps. Like the heart
after the gods have had their fill, what's left
after our banquet of loss.

When Samy got sick,
he'd turn on the radio
the moment he was alone
Music. News. Even white noise.

He would have hated it here
the field shrouded in fog
only a smattering
of birdsong.

He was twenty-eight.
I've lived long enough
to count my dead
on both hands.

Some days
I sit and listen
to the tic of the clock,
the rustle of the nuthatch
gathering bark for her nest.

And just beyond, a silence
so pristine,
that if I hold my breath
here they are, again,
returned, shy deer
at the forest's edge.

LADY IN SATIN

It's come to this, again.
I've returned to her
let myself back
into the darkness

of her voice,
slipping
on the notes
while the band plays
so slow
they sound underwater.

I want to reach
into the river
she is drowning in
pull her up
by the bare shoulder
above her ruined gown.

But every time
I play the record
she touches the white gardenia
opening behind her ear
says because of him
her world is bright.

Although I know
the story, I keep listening.
Even if she could
she wouldn't save me.

UNDER THE REDWOODS

I unbutton my blouse
offer my lover
breasts, still heavy with milk.
My husband is gone
the last of his belongings
heaped in the garage.

This man
I hardly know
lowers his face
takes the dark nipple
in his mouth.

Somewhere in the trees
above our heads
a blue jay cries out
its sharp complaint,
while down the path
a horse gallops creekside
hooves grazing
the flat stones.

Around us
thousand-year old trunks
hold winter light.
A swarm of gnats
hovers in midair.

I feel a cool hand
slip around my waist
and then that odd
familiar ache
just before the milk lets down.

Earthquakes, flood, fire.
How is it anything endures?
The dome of the Parthenon
encircling its shaft of afternoon light.
Marble statues poised in mid-gait
beneath the Roman sun.
Deer and buffalo drawn in ochre
on the walls of caves.
And here, shards of pottery,
sandals placed beside the body
of a Pharaoh
who waits to enter
the next kingdom, bones
buried in catacombs,
a woman's pelvis
the three children she bore
evidenced along the frail rim, insects
articulated in amber.
Sappho's fragments
still clinging to papyrus
He is a god who sits beside you . . .
Letters passed between lovers
in a language long extinct.
After we have loved each other
isn't there something that remains?
A faint scrawl
on the parchment of the heart,
blurred, illegible,
a relic of an empire.

three

REMODELING

My brother was in the middle
of remodeling the bathroom
the summer he shot himself.
He'd ripped out the old fixtures,
left remnants on the dusty floor:
the stump of a broken sink
sitting among caulk guns
and six penny nails,
a diamond-edged saw.

Each day, he'd kneel down
to the task,
the wiring of his brain
shaking loose. He cut
sleek marble tile
stacked it in the corner
his beautiful arms
muscled, taut.
Sometimes he sang to himself.
Sometimes it was all he could do
to keep his hands steady,
keep from wandering
that far country
traveling its disheveled boulevards.

Holding a Philips-head
in his hand, he'd smile, kiss
our mother on the cheek

when she brought him lunch.
Now, sunlight pours into that room
sounds its dull echo
off porcelain and chrome.

He'd become a stranger to us.

Imagine them going ahead
into the afterlife
like the first guests
at a cocktail party.
They slip their insubstantial bodies
into elegant attire,
down drinks of ether
and dance to the rhythm of the spheres.

The night they spill into
is always warm, the music fine.

And when one of their companions departs,
it's never to die
but to be born—to enter the thick
darkness of the womb
set foot on the green earth.

But quiet now,
as they lift their glasses, make a toast
to the guest of honor
who has not yet arrived,
but rests deep in her sunken pillow
about to rasp
her final lungful of air
before stepping out of her costume of skin
into a gown of stars.

ANYTHING

Anything could happen in our father's house
that rusted, half-built tower of redwood
perched at the edge of the Pacific
where my brother and I spent summers
and Christmases, our dad playing Beethoven,
on the rickety stereo, making red wine,
dancing in the bathtub on the broken skins.
At night, in the cricket-loud dark,
raccoons tore wet peelings from the kitchen trash
while I lay in bed, bone still, caught the draft
off the wings of bats as they whirled crazily in the rafters.
By morning, visitors appeared, unbidden:
a woman named Moon shed her clothes at the door,
then lay naked in the garden by the zucchini.
Preacher Mike rolled out his pungent herbs on thin
white paper, crying, *the Lord is my shepherd,*
I shall not want. Once, in a gale, a young owl
took shelter on the porch and stayed for weeks.
I heard people talk: *that crazy Dutchman*
and his two black kids. Look at them bent over
a pile of bricks, laying mortar in the midday sun.
But what could I do? When the work was done
my brother and I made boats of scrap wood, then knelt
by the gutter and sailed them in the runoff.
We watched as they hobbled down the dirty stream
and then, we hoped, to the sea.

Under the watchful eyes of their captors
they passed the hours,
a man, his wife, deep in the jungle.
Sometimes they were allowed
to forage for food
finding only sticky grains
of infested rice.
At night they slept,
handcuffed to a tree.

When at last they were alone,
they talked long into the afternoon.
He didn't want to hear how much
she loved him, that whatever happened . . .
Instead they planned their family trips
in great detail.

If, for example, they traveled
from Raleigh to Memphis,
how many hours would it take?
How many gallons of gas?
They would pack each child's suitcase
in their minds, line them up at the door
and lower them, gingerly,
into the trunk.

Then do it all over again in reverse,
as if they couldn't get enough of it:

the price of gas per gallon,
a child's small t-shirt, crumpled
at the bottom of a bag,
the back seat littered with popcorn,
plastic cups, Kleenex,
the long gray freeway
with its endless signs.

INTERVIEW

for Temple Grandin

She said it was because she could think like a cow.
That maybe the autism helped her understand
how to design the curved corrals
so they'd flow more easily through the gates.

The harness that held the dairy cow waiting to be milked
made sense to her. She wanted to be inside it, to feel the world
pressing away, something not a human touch.

"Do you feel emotions," the interviewer asked, leaning against the barn.
"Joy? Sadness? What about love?" She shook her head and turned
toward the last few stragglers in the stall
as the camera panned across her face
into the broad Texas sky.

"I don't know," she said, "but I think love must be like this,
when all the cattle are moving in the right direction,
and they're not afraid."

The woman at the party slipped him in my arms
so she could fix herself a plate of food. Sometimes
this happens—a mother with brown skin, an island voice
will see in me her own mother, her sister,
a tributary of the blue river that runs through her veins.
But this baby was so new, his eyes still bloodshot from birth,
the red spreading like a stain through the sclera's milky white.
I held his swaddled body while he stretched those thin,
alien fingers, then clenched them back into the flannel caul.
From time to time he squinted up at me, this woman
in whose arms, for a moment, his life rested.
He did not cry, though now and then
his mouth moved in that familiar gesture of hunger.
And I did not dare sit, for fear he would disapprove,
my knees remembering the boat-like bobbing
that the new-to-land prefer. I looked down
at his squinched face, the whispered trace of eyebrows,
delicate folds of his lids, black hair, curls fine
as the whorled loops of a fingerprint,
and I wanted to whisper into his intricate ear
tell him the lie I couldn't make true:
that this is a world where he will always be safe
in the arms of a stranger. Even as he grows tall
in the darkness of his skin,
he can walk down any street, day or night,
feet scuffing the rough ground,
hands in his pockets,
his heart, whole, in his chest.

Oh Etta, you are not done singing.
Not in the shower, not anywhere.

In the world inside my stereo
it is 1946, and I can see you, still
lit by the orange sundown
holding a small glass of bourbon
in your languid fingers
wrist bent in soft
surrender to its weight.

You are leaning back
into the florid afternoon, Etta,
and I say *tell it girl,*
tell us all the bad things
beauty's made of.

for Samy

I took the warm towel, dipped in antiseptic
and swabbed the side of his face,
his skin throbbing from the heat
his body was making.
Then down his sternum,
slow around the plastic tube
that disappeared into a hole
beside his heart.
It felt good to touch him,
the wet cloth skimming his chest.
He closed his eyes, not wanting,
I imagine, to see me seeing him like that
but also because of the pleasure of it.
He knew, by then, to take what was good:
the quiet room, the shadows of trees
on the walls, the woman
leaning over him, attentive, purposeful.
Almost a painting, the way the light fell
on his face, the profile
I remember from our first dance,
lips he pressed
to the back of my hand.
What kindness, the light
and its careful shadows.
It seemed, for just a while longer
we could have stayed this way,
his breath, steadied, even.

They are ordinary, here. The man
lying in the metal bed
a mask over his face, his eyes
unfocused, his head smooth,
the woman looking down at him,
her hand in his, keeping pace
with the stranger
in loose green clothing
who pushes the bed toward the elevator.
There are spectators,
a group of them,
waiting for the doors to slick open
then close.

And now this woman,
silently calling out to the man—
Romeo, Romeo—
as if she could summon him
from the depths of the morphine,
that elegant darkness.

Do they ever want to escape?
Climb out of the white pages
and enter our world?

Holden Caulfield slipping in the movie theater
to catch the two o'clock.
Anna Karenina sitting in a diner,
reading the paper as the waitress
serves up a cheeseburger.

Even Hector, on break from the Iliad,
takes a stroll through the park,
admires the tulips.

Maybe they grew tired
of the author's mind,
all its twists and turns.

Or were finally weary
of stumbling around Pamplona,
a bottle in each fist,
eating lotuses on the banks of the Nile.

For others, it was just too hot
in the small California town
where they'd been written into
a lifetime of plowing fields.

Whatever the reason,
here they are, roaming the city streets
rain falling on their phantasmal shoulders.

Wouldn't you, if you could?
Step out of your own story,
to lean against a doorway
of the Five & Dime, sipping your coffee,

your life, somewhere far behind you,
all its heat and toil nothing but a tale
resting in the hands of a stranger,
the sidewalk ahead wet and glistening.

The past is right there.
I can see that man and that woman.
They're us.
They're sitting in the deli.
It's lunchtime. They're laughing
and talking but they can't see me
or hear me knock on the glass.
"Hello?" "Hello?"
I want a word with them.
I want to tell them *don't do it.*
Don't have the child
whose life will hang by a strand.
You will hate each other for it.
But they look so happy
sitting at that table
half-way through
a pastrami sandwich
drinking root beer,
my voice locks
in my throat.

Often, when I think of him now,
I think of his body
lying at the bottom
of that rough dirt hole
his handsome face turned
toward the side
his mouth, open slightly
a few dense curls
showing through his white shroud.
As though all of us
had just caught him sleeping
and he was unaware of the crowd.
In fact, he didn't wake
when some wailed or cried out
and others chanted prayers.
Not when we began to gather clods of dirt
and throw them on his body
on his quiet face.
Not when the hole filled in
with shovel-fulls of dirt.
No. He was undisturbed by the living
all our heat and sweat and sound.
Not even the sun would wake him now
its relentless rising in the east
persistent as love
steady as despair.

four

ELEVEN

That was the year they began, those terrible
crushes on girls. Girls already in eighth grade
who wore tight sweaters and opalescent eye shadow
who we watched in the hallways, their hips pressed
to the narrow pelvises of boys, the straps of their tank tops
sliding off their bronzed shoulders.
How we envied them their broken curfews
and chipped nail polish, their curved calves and
feathered bangs, had seen them
stand before the mirror in the littered bathroom aisle
lick their lavender gloss, then look up
towards the harsh fluorescent lights
and raise a tilted wand to their lashes.
And when they walked, the air behind them swayed,
heady with flowers and the scent
of their own ripening. It seemed impossible, then
that we would become them.
Whatever language it was they spoke,
clustered together, leaning in,
before they broke apart in scattered cries,
it was theirs alone. Even now
they float before me, ambassadors of beauty,
twisting strands of shiny hair
around their slender fingers,
chewing spearmint gum as they
scratch initials into their wooden desks,
staring out the windows
peering through us
into the life that lay ahead.

We rode all afternoon along the barren creek bed
jumping boulders, kicking up dust, clutching the coarse manes.
I wrapped my thin thighs around the bulging sides
and hung on. It didn't matter there were horse flies,
heat, the itch against our legs, the dry grass full of ticks
and ready to catch fire. We were ten years old and flying
past fields fringed with oak and aspen, held skyward—
the earth, its rough stones and clumps of nettle—
weightless below. For a while, we'd forget
our spiral notebooks covered in glittered stickers,
the careful shape of the words we etched inside,
the sardine can of the yellow bus where boys
elbowed us in the ribs, grazing the small cones of our breasts.
Whatever it was our fathers drank from the bottles
they kept above the sink, whatever our mothers cursed
as they soaked the dirty dishes, straightened the sheets,
we were beyond it now, crashing down into the empty creek,
only to lift back up into the summer air.
We were that light, that far outside the laws of gravity.
Nothing could touch us.

I was twenty when my mother took me to see him.
He was French, silver-haired. He held my arm,
lifted it to his aquiline nose, sniffed
the inside of my slender wrist
then nodded, scrawled
a few things on a slip of parchment
in that Gallic hand: Rose Absolute, Ambergris.
I wish I could remember more. Then one-by-one,
picked up the bottles, decanted viscous honey
into a slim blue vial. I touched the mouth
of the vessel to my skin, inhaled.

I wore it that whole year, the sweet musk,
under a sweater on my way to class,
over the soft pulse in my neck
where men pressed their lips.
And when my friend's mother died,
I wore it to her funeral.
It carried me, a sort of cloud
I breathed, a balm of certainty.
Now, all that's left, an absence, distilled,
fragrance of longing, that ache
we walk with all our lives.

My mother once had a job measuring penises—
penises that belonged to men whose chromosomes
were askew. "The trouble," she said,
"is that when I went to measure them, they'd grow!"
I picture her pulling a wooden ruler
from a pocket in her white lab coat.
How hard we try to break the world down,
make sense of it. How steadily it resists.
My friend David, an astrophysicist,
had a job counting the clouds of dust around stars,
an assignment that, in my mind,
put him in an echelon of angels
just above the ones who number grains of sand.
There's something comforting about inventory,
futile as it may be, the act of assessment,
itself, a form of care. I like to imagine a God
who rises before dawn, takes out the stone tablets,
and starts to tally the individual hairs on each head,
the number of breaths we've taken in the night,
who counts the cilia shooting our cells
through the dark galaxies of our bodies
just before he gets back to work
turning out the next tornado
or reaching down to give the tectonic plates
another good, hard shake.

It lands on the white page
right under the glare of my flashlight
and I'm startled, not by the idea of a fly
soiling the last section of Jack Gilbert's poem,
its furred legs obscuring the lines about the ancient
Sumerian tablets not being inventory, but poems or psalms.
It's the beauty that surprises me, a kind of iridescence
I'd imagine reserved for Cleopatra's jewels.
Though what gem glitters so? In the alphabet
of veridity I can name, emerald, malachite
serpentine, jade. But this is green fused with gold
the way Thai silk glimmers two different shades,
depending on how you hold it to the light,
or the dipped-in-liquid color
painted inside an abalone shell.
Peacocks know this hue, luminosity reflected
off their satin tail feathers.
I wish I could be a fly on the wall, we say.
I have swatted flies, shooed them out the window,
brushed them from my arms in the heat of summer.
But this one rustles its filigreed wings, shifts its body,
now covering the words, "ingots," and "copper"
and for a moment I see it—held aloft
by the bezel of language—looking back at me
through its big, glossy black eye.

LONE WOLF

*On December 28, 2011, the first wolf in nearly a hundred years was seen
crossing the border of the Sierra Nevada from Oregon to California.*

A male, probably looking for a mate
in this high wilderness
along the cusp of Mount Shasta.
Already there are ranchers waiting, armed.
True, it's only one wolf.
Except that a wolf is never just a wolf.
We say "wolf" but mean our own hunger,
walking around outside our bodies.
The thief desire is. The part of wanting
we want to forget but can't. Not
with the wolf loose in the woods
carrying the thick fur
of our longing. Not with it taking
in its mouth the flocks we keep
penned behind barbed wire.
If only we didn't have to hear it
out in the dark, howling.

THE OLDEST LIVING THING

Somewhere in the White Mountains of California,
older than Christ, the Buddha, a bristlecone pine
has stood for nearly five thousand years
on a ridge now covered with trees—
can they be called trees? More corporeal
than we think trees to be: gristle, sinew,
the gnarled hands of a biblical god.
Except that they reach skyward,
their edict directed to the heavens.
Could they be petitioning on our behalf?
This world is so heavy with grief.
Do they reverberate each time
a bomb explodes, a species goes extinct?
Or are they immune to all the endless suffering?
One has stood longer than the pyramids,
perched in the dry soil, taking in the clean
or tainted air, the sharp blades
of sun, bird song, whatever rain falls.

Don't you wish they would stop,
all the thoughts swirling around in your head,
bees in a hive, dancers tapping their way across the stage.
I should rake the leaves in the carport, buy Christmas lights.
Was there really life on Mars? What will I cook for dinner?
I walk up the driveway, put out the garbage bins.
I should stop using plastic bags, visit my friend
whose husband just left her for the Swedish nanny.
I wish I hadn't said Patrick's painting looked, "ominous."
Maybe that's why he hasn't called.
Does the car need oil, again? There's a hole in the ozone
the size of Texas and everything seems to be speeding up.
Come, let's stand by the window and look out
at the light on the field. Let's watch how
the clouds cover the sun and almost nothing
stirs in the grass.

WHAT I DIDN'T DO

I never called her back, the woman
with the two babies born just like mine.
Girls who couldn't crawl or talk,
could barely smile, who lay there,
bundled in flowered dresses, staring
at the ceiling. Both had lovely,
extravagant names, like opera singers
or stars of the ballet. She wanted,
I imagine, to sit with me—
the only woman she knew
like her, drink coffee,
stir it with silver spoons
as the steam rose to our tired eyes
and our babies lay there, inert
and beautiful, sucking their small hands.
Was it so much to ask? She'd written
her number on a slip of paper,
put it in my palm. And week after week,
I promised myself to triumph
in this one, small thing,
pictured her lifting the girls
into their beds at night, the way I did
my son. Or dropping the bitter
medicines into their open mouths
perhaps alone, afraid. I did what
villagers have done for centuries,
when they shun the widow,
the man with one eye.
Hadn't lightning struck her twice?
I turned my back, kept her luck
from being added to mine.

My nephew still wears a trace
of his baby smell.
When I pull his gangly body
towards me, inhale the scent
wafting from his crown
there's just the slightest whiff.
"I know," he says when I mention it,
twisting back and forth in my arms.

Only last year he stopped lisping his s's.
Sometimes in front of his friends
he pretends not to know us.

Love's a record keeper:
baby teeth, first wisps of hair,
growth marks inked on the wall.
We know we're going to lose everything.

She was at a friend's apartment,
my mother, a third floor walk-up.
It was summer. Why she slipped
into the back room, she can't recall.
Was there something she wanted
from her purse . . . lipstick?
a phone number?
Fumbling through the pile
on the bed she looked up and saw—
was this possible?—outside,
on the thin concrete ledge
a child, a girl, no more than two or three.
She was crouched down
eyeing an object with great interest.
A pebble, or a bright coin.
What happened next
must have happened very slowly.
My mother, who was young then,
leaned out the window, smiled.
Would you like to see
what's in my purse? she asked.
Below, traffic rushed
down the wide street, horns blaring.
Students ambled home
under the weight of their backpacks.
From the next room,
strains of laughter.
The child smiled back, toddled along

the ledge. What do we know
of fate or chance, the threads
that hold us in the balance?
My mother did not imagine
one day she would
lose her own son, helpless
to stop the bullet
he aimed at his heart.
She reached out to the girl,
grabbed her in both arms,
held her to her chest.

ASHES

for my son

What his body was becoming across town
while I washed dishes, slept, brought in the mail.
I even ate ice cream, holding the cold
to my lips, trying not to picture it, the way
the body rises, alarmed, at the first rush of heat.

What I carried later in a blue lacquer box
a butterfly on the lid, slipped into my purse,
reached down and held. It could have been a compact,
dust to tint the cheeks. Ash grey, ashen.
The way I must have looked walking
through the market, past the eggs and milk,
down the narrow aisles of the living.

The woman standing in the Whole Foods aisle
over the pyramid of fruit, neatly arranged
under glossy lights, watched me drop
a handful into a paper bag, said how do you do it?
I always have to check each one.
I looked down at the dark red fruit, each cherry
good in its own, particular way
the way breasts are good or birds or stars.
Doesn't everything that shines carry its own shadow?
A scar across the surface, a worm buried in the sweet flesh.
Why not reach in, take whatever falls into your hand.

HORSE

Is it better to call it "the Tao" rather than "God"? You could call it "the horse."

—Byron Katie

Let us offer sheaves of wheat to its soft mouth
gallop bareback, holding fast the rough mane.

"Whatever the horse brings"
"Arabian," "Azteca" "Appaloosa"

forelock, muzzle,
hock and hoof

A child is born
"horse"

A building burns down
"horse"

There is a field. There are horses,
some dark, some dappled,

some visible only in clouds.

At night, moving
across the shadow of the moon.

ACKNOWLEDGMENTS

The following poems have appeared in the journals listed, sometimes in slightly different versions:

Alaska Quarterly Review: "Pigeons," "Under the Redwoods," "The Moons of August"

Atlanta Review: "What Trees Dream Of," "The Dead,"(as "The Dead I've Loved"), "The Perfumer"

Caesura: "Remodeling"

Cold Mountain Review: "Eleven," "What Remains"

Connotation Press: "Horse"

Lyric: "Sing It," "Lady in Satin"

Memoir: "The Balance," "The Bath"

phren-Z: "Silence," "Nina," "When Mary Wept," "Riding Bareback" (winner of the 2013 Morton Marcus Memorial Poetry Contest, selected by Gary Young)

Poet Lore: "Hostages"

Porter Gulch Review: "Apples"

Rattle: "The Lord God Bird," "Arabic"

Red Wheelbarrow: "My Brother," "A Square of White," "The Oldest Living Thing"

The Sun Magazine: "Fictional Characters," "Eve, After," "Names," "What I Didn't Do," "The God of Numbers," "Thinking"

The Syracuse Cultural Workers: "Cherries"

The Undaunted Dove: "I Have Been That Woman"

Water~Stone: "Interview"

"Crows" (as "The Crows Return") appeared in the anthology *A Bird Black as the Sun: California Poets on Crows and Ravens*. "Act One" appeared in the anthology *In a Fine Frenzy: Poets Respond to Shakespeare*.

I am grateful to many people who have supported the creation of this manuscript: The Wednesday afternoon writers of years gone by, my students for keeping me on my toes. The Squaw Valley Community of Writers. My dear friends Susan-Jane Harrison, and Madeleine Schulman. Poem companion Dane Cervine. The P. Gurlz: Farnaz Fatemi, Lisa Allen Ortiz, Ingrid Moody LaRiviere and Frances Hatfield, for feedback served with wine and chocolate. Alice Simon Gabriel, Arthur Ward, and Tony Hoagland for starting me on the path. My grandfather, Gordon Bell, for paving the way. My family for their support. Dorianne Laux and Joseph Millar for their extraordinary wit and input. Ellen Bass for her ongoing mentorship—as a person, a teacher, and a poet. Gratitude to Autumn House Press and to Naomi Shihab Nye for choosing this manuscript. Thank you! And especially, my husband, Armando, for his bottomless encouragement and for giving me the space and time to write.

The Autumn House Poetry Series

Michael Simms, General Editor

OneOnOne	Jack Myers
Snow White Horses	Ed Ochester
The Leaving	Sue Ellen Thompson
Dirt	Jo McDougall
Fire in the Orchard	Gary Margolis
Just Once: New and Previous Poems	Samuel Hazo
The White Calf Kicks	Deborah Slicer • 2003, selected by Naomi Shihab Nye
The Divine Salt	Peter Blair
The Dark Takes Aim	Julie Suk
Satisfied with Havoc	Jo McDougall
Half Lives	Richard Jackson
Not God After All	Gerald Stern
Dear Good Naked Morning	Ruth L. Schwartz • 2004, selected by Alicia Ostriker
A Flight to Elsewhere	Samuel Hazo
Collected Poems	Patricia Dobler
The Autumn House Anthology of Contemporary American Poetry	Sue Ellen Thompson, ed.
Déjà Vu Diner	Leonard Gontarek
lucky wreck	Ada Limón • 2005, selected by Jean Valentine
The Golden Hour	Sue Ellen Thompson
Woman in the Painting	Andrea Hollander Budy
Joyful Noise: An Anthology of American Spiritual Poetry	Robert Strong, ed.
No Sweeter Fat	Nancy Pagh • 2006, selected by Tim Seibles

Shelter	Gigi Marks*
The Autumn House Anthology of Contemporary American Poetry, 2nd ed.	Michael Simms, ed.
To Make It Right	Corrinne Clegg Hales • 2010, selected by Claudia Emerson
The Torah Garden	Philip Terman
Lie Down with Me	Julie Suk
The Beds	Martha Rhodes
The Water Books	Judith Vollmer
Sheet Music	Robert Gibb
Natural Causes	Brian Brodeur • 2011, selected by Denise Duhamel
Miraculum	Ruth L. Schwartz
Late Rapturous	Frank X. Gaspar
Bathhouse Betty	Matt Terhune*
Irish Coffee	Jay Carson*
A Raft of Grief	Chelsea Rathburn • 2012, selected by Stephen Dunn
A Poet's Sourcebook: Writings about Poetry, from the Ancient World to the Present	Dawn Potter, ed.
Landscape with Female Figure: New and Selected Poems, 1982–2002	Andrea Hollander
Prayers of an American Wife	Victoria Kelly*
Rooms of the Living	Paul Martin*
Mass of the Forgotten	James Tolan
The Moons of August	Danusha Laméris • 2013, selected by Naomi Shihab Nye

• Winner of the annual Autumn House Poetry Prize

* *Coal Hill Review* chapbook series

DESIGN AND PRODUCTION

Text and cover design: Chiquita Babb

Cover painting: Melissa Melero, "Awommo's Paumma"

Author photograph: Mark Stover, Expressive Photographics

This book is typeset in Adobe Jenson, an oldstyle font designed by Robert
Slimbach, with Roman characters based on a Venetian font designed by
Nicholas Jenson in 1470, and italics based on the early sixteenth century
italics of Ludovico degli Arrighi da Vicenza. Display elements are set in Weiss,
a font designed in the Renaissance Chancery script style by Emil Rudolf
Weiss in 1926.

This book was printed by McNaughton & Gunn on 55# Glatfelter Natural.